WELCOME TO THE ANCIENT FAR NORTH . . . AND THE WORLD OF THE MICEKINGS!

WHERE THEY LIVE: Miceking Island

CAPITAL: Mouseborg, home of the Stiltonord family

OTHER VILLAGES: Oofadale, village of the Oofa Oofas, and Feargard, village of the vilekings

CLIMATE: Cold, cold, cold, especially when the icy north wind blows!

TYPICAL FOOD: Gloog, a superstinky but fabumouse stew. The secret recipe is closely guarded by the wife of the miceking chief.

NATIONAL DRINK: Finnbrew, made of equal parts codfish juice and herring juice, with a splash of squid ink

MEANS OF TRANSPORTATION: The drekar, a light but very fast ship

GREATEST HONOR: The miceking helmet. It is only earned when a mouse performs an act of courage or wins a Miceking Challenge.

UNIT OF MEASUREMENT: A mouseking tail (full tail, half tail, third tail, quarter tail)

ENEMIES: The terrible dragons who live in Beastgard

MEET THE STILTONORD FAMILY ...

GERONIMO
Advisor to the
miceking chief

THEA
A horse trainer who
works well with all kinds
of animals

TRAP
The most famouse
inventor in Mouseborg

BENJAMIN
Geronimo's nephew

BUGSILDA
Benjamin's best
friend

. . . AND THE EVIL DRAGONS!

The dragons are divided into 5 clans, all of which are terrifying!

1. Devourers
They love to eat micekings raw — no cooking necessary.

2. Steamers
They grab micekings, then fly over volcanoes so the steam and smoke make them taste good.

SIZZLE
The cook

3. Biters
Before eating micekings, they nibble them delicately to see if they like them or not.

4. Slurpers
They wrap their long tongues around micekings and slurp them up.

5. Rinsers
As soon as they catch micekings, they rinse them in a stream to wash them off.

Geronimo Stilton

MICEKINGS

STAY STRONG, GERONIMO!

Scholastic Inc.

Published by Scholastic Inc., *Publishers since 1920*, 557 Broadway, New York, NY 10012. SCHOLASTIC and associated logos are trademarks and/or registered trademarks of Scholastic Inc.

ISBN 978-1-338-08869-4

Text by Geronimo Stilton
Original title *La rivincita delle topinghe!*
Cover by Giuseppe Facciotto (pencils) and Flavio Ferron (ink and color)
Illustrations by Giuseppe Facciotto (pencils) and Alessandro Costa (ink and color)
Graphics by Chiara Cebraro

Special thanks to Tracey West
Translated by Emily Clement
Interior design by Becky James

10 9 8 7 6 5 4 3 2 1   17 18 19 20 21   .

Printed in the U.S.A.   40
First printing 2017

DRAGON ALERT!

It was a splendid fall morning in Mouseborg, the capital of Miceking Island. The colorful leaves waved in the gentle breeze.

Most micekings are **WARRIORS**, but I don't like fighting. I decided to sneak away for a walk in the woods. There, I would find inspiration in nature, and —

Sorry, I haven't introduced myself! My name is *GERONIMO STILTONORD*, and I am a mouseking and a SCHOLAR.

That morning, I was a hungry

scholar! I filled my backpack with **one** small barrel of fjordberry juice, **two** loaves of bread, and **THREE** wheels of super-stinky Stenchberg cheese.

At the last minute, I added cheese wheel number **FOUR**. Physical exercise gives me a **big appetite**!

I whistled as I headed toward the woods. I strolled until I found myself in a silent **CLEARING** surrounded by nature.

But before I could unpack my picnic, the sound of a horn rose up from Three Lookouts Cliff.

TOO-TOOT! TOO-TOOOOOOOOT!

Squeak! It was the *dragon alarm*!

TOO-TOOOOOOOT!
TOO-TOOOOOOOT!

Oh no! Dragons!

THE SHIELD MOUSELET MEGA CHALLENGE

When the dragon alarm sounded, everyone in the village was supposed to run to face the dragons. Did I mention that the dragons are **FIERCE** and terrible and always starving for **fresh** miceking meat?

I ran back through the woods and *RUSHED* to the village in record miceking speed. When I arrived at the Great Stone Square, the other micekings were already there.

"**Draaagons!**" I yelled.

Oddly, nobody else was yelling. Or **running** for the catapults. I ran over to

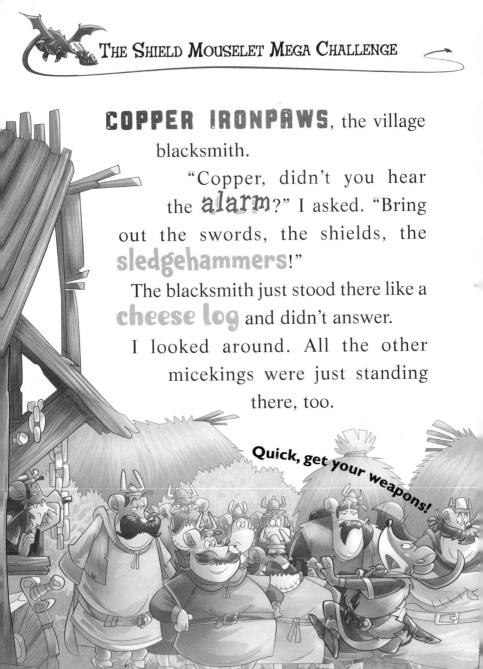

COPPER IRONPAWS, the village blacksmith.

"Copper, didn't you hear the **alarm**?" I asked. "Bring out the swords, the shields, the **sledgehammers**!"

The blacksmith just stood there like a **cheese log** and didn't answer.

I looked around. All the other micekings were just standing there, too.

Quick, get your weapons!

"Holey cheese!" I shouted. "Why isn't anybody getting ready to **fight** the dragons?"

Nobody answered me.

"What is **WRONG** with you rodents?" I asked.

Then **SVEN THE SHOUTER**, our village leader, marched up to me.

"Geronimo, you smarty-mouseking!" he shouted. (He always **SHOUTS**. How do you think he got his name?) "Here you are at last!"

"Sven! The d-d-d-dragons!" I stuttered.

He smacked my back with his massive paw. "There aren't any dragons, you mollusk! We sounded the alarm to get you out of your hiding place."

"I wasn't hiding," I protested.

Go sit down!

"Spare me the **EXCUSES**, smarty-paws," he said. "We've been **LOOKING** all over for you. It's time to start the competition!"

"COMPETITION? What competition?" I asked.

"Horns and thorns, don't be a CHEESEHEAD! Just go sit in your spot at the judges' table. That's an order!" Sven shouted.

"SO SAYS SVEN THE SHOUTER!"

the other micekings yelled.

I sighed. So much for my picnic!

Only then did I notice that a **stage** had been built in the village square. It was decorated *festively*. But, by my whiskers, I couldn't think of what competition

8

could be happening that day.

The **GREAT BEARD CHALLENGE** to determine the mouseking with the thickest beard had been a few weeks earlier.

The **Stinky Codfish Festival** was always held the first week of spring.

The **MICEKING GAMES**, which attracted micekings from all over the island, were planned for the summer.

So . . . this must be the **Shield Mouselet Mega Challenge**! Female warrior micekings are known as Shield Mouselets. Each fall, they compete to see who is the **BRAVEST**, **strongest**, and **smartest**.

Everyone loved the challenge — except me! Sven always made me judge, and it always got me in **BIG TROUBLE**.

After I took my seat, my cousin **Trap** slid into the chair next to me.

"Trap, are you on the judges' panel, too?" I asked.

He chuckled. "Of course! A judge has to understand COURAGE, **strength**, and intelligence. And since I am brave, strong, and smart, I'll be the PERFECT judge!"

We heard an amused laugh behind us and turned to see a large female mouseking: RATILDE. "If anyone can judge the COURAGE of a mouseking, it's me!" she boasted as she sat down in the third judge's chair.

Trap and I nodded. Ratilde was captain of the ship Beauty of the Seas, and there wasn't a single mouseking sailor who was **BRAVER** than her.*

"We all need courage to judge this contest,"

* To read more about Ratilde, check out my adventure *The Famouse Fjord Race!*

THORA

Sven the Shouter's daughter is charming, brave, and good at everything she tries — and I have a big crush on her!

HELGA

She is as sweet as she is strong — and she makes Trap blush.

I whispered to them both.

"Why?" Trap asked.

"Because there can only be one winner," I replied. "And then we are left with angry losers!"

Just then, I saw that **Thora** was a contestant this year. She is SVEN'S daughter — and my **secret crush**. I gulped. I had to pick Thora as the winner, right?

The other CONTESTANTS were Helga, Karina,

and my sister, Thea.

I GULPED again. How could I vote against Helga, who is so **STRONG**? Or Karina, the *FASTEST* mouseking around? Or my own talented sister, Thea?

I could smell trouble already . . . but then I smelled something else. Something very strong.

I sniffed the air. "What is that strange stench?" I asked.

Ratilde snorted and passed me a clothespin

Karina

This mouseking is fast, agile, and does everything with flair.

THEA

My sister, Thea, is a brilliant rodent! She loves adventure and competitions.

What a smell!

to put on my nose. "Here you go, you wimpy mouseking!" she said.

Then I saw that the smell was coming from the braided sash that would be awarded to the winning Shield Mouselet. It was made out of **hot peppers**! Rotten ricotta, those peppers had such a *STRONG SCENT* that they were making my eyes water!

Ratilde nudged me. "Look, smarty-mouseking, even Trap has **WATERY** eyes."

14

"It's not the peppers," Trap said.

Then I noticed that Helga was smiling at him. My big cousin has such a **tender** heart!

Logi Peppers

Logi peppers are very strong hot peppers that are used in our famouse miceking hot pepper sauce, the hottest sauce there is! These peppers have a much, much, much stronger smell than even stinky miceking garlic.

BEGIN THE MEGA CHALLENGES!

Sven the Shouter climbed onto the stage. "Citizens of Mouseborg, hear me!" he shouted. "Only the **BRAVEST**, **strongest**, and **smartest** contestant will win the Shield Mouselet Mega Challenge!"

"SO SAYS SVEN THE SHOUTER!"

the crowd cheered.

Sven raised his paw in the air. "Let the competition begin!"

The first event was the **shell challenge**. Each contestant had to throw a RAZOR-SHARP shell at a straw target.

SHIVERING SQUIDS!

Those shells had points as sharp as DRAGONS' CLAWS.

Thea's shell passed so close to me that it trimmed the ends of my whiskers! But she hit the bull's-eye and won the contest.

Bull's-eye!

My whiskers!

The second event was the **rope challenge**.

Miceking ships need good, strong ropes to set their **powerful** sails. The contestants had to **quickly** braid ropes to see who could make the longest rope at the fastest **SPEED**.

My job was to measure to see who braided

I need more rope!

I'm all tangled up!

the **longest** rope. I tried my best, but I got all **tangled up**! I nearly tripped and fell flat on my snout!

Finally, I untangled myself and measured the long braids. And the **WINNER** of the rope challenge was . . .

...**Karina**! Her rope was three hundred tails long!

Next up was the cooking challenge.

Every mouseking worth his or her helmet needs to know how to make **hearty** food out of whatever is handy. Miceking food has to be **delicious** and **nutritious** enough to build big miceking muscles!

"This is my *favorite* challenge," Trap said, rubbing his belly.

Algae and mussels

Moldy moss from
Saltwater Valley

The contestants had to **cook** a dish out of these common ingredients:

1. **Algae** and **mussels**
2. Moldy **moss** from Saltwater Valley
3. 100-year-old smoked **HERRING**
4. Rancid **CODFISH** fat
5. Logi pepper **cheese**

The three judges had to **taste** each dish and rate it on how **nutritious** and

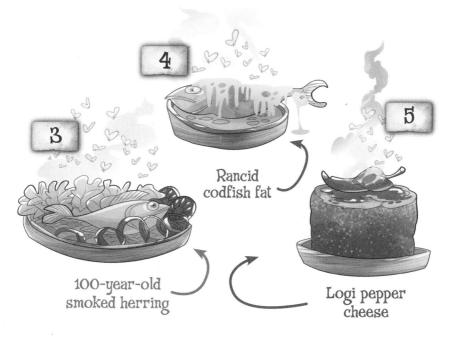

Rancid codfish fat

100-year-old smoked herring

Logi pepper cheese

delicious it was. Thea presented her dish first. It smelled awful!

Now, I know my sister well. She is brave, athletic, and great with animals. But she is a terrible cook!

"Um, I'm not hungry," I said, pushing it away.

Thea frowned. "Are you going to judge it or not, Geronimo?"

Yuck! How gross!

Trap slapped my back. "Eat up, Cousin! What are you afraid of?"

I had to eat the dish in order to fairly judge the contest.

I took one bite of deep-fried aged herring in **stinky cheese sauce** and swallowed.

My stomach went **UP** and **DOWN**, **UP** and **DOWN**, **UP** and **DOWN**!

"You look a little **green**, Geronimo," Trap remarked. "Did you eat too much? No problem. Ratilde and I will take care of the rest."

I was very **lucky** that Trap and Ratilde had **cast-iron** stomachs! They declared **Thora** the winner. I wanted to congratulate her, but I couldn't.

My stomach hurt so much . . .

I WAS AFRAID I MIGHT TOSS MY CHEESE!

So, Who Is the Winner?

The next event was the **cauldron challenge**, a test of **strength** and **balance**. Each Shield Mouselet had to perform a complicated dance while balancing a heavy cauldron full of swamp water on her head.

Thea DRAGGED me from the judges' table to dance with her. [1] She SPUN me around and around like a top!

Spin!
Spin!

Squeak!

1

1

2 We **TWIRLED** and twirled in circles. I got dizzy and fell against Thea . . . **BAM!**

3 I knocked into the cauldron, and all the swamp water dumped on my head!

Faster!

Stop!

2

AAAAAAAH!

HELGA kept the cauldron on her head the longest, and she **won** the challenge.

3

Oh no!

Aaaah!

The four contestants were tied. Everything depended on the final event: the **CAMOUFLAGE CHALLENGE**. Camouflage is an important skill when facing an **ENEMY** or hiding from miceking-eating **dragons**. For this event, the Shield Mouselets had to create an outfit that would work as camouflage in the **ocean**.

Thora dove into the sea and found a big **shell** for her outfit.

I found a shell!

The four contestants put together their camouflage and stood onstage. Everyone cheered for them loudly.

"GO, THEA!"
"THORA IS THE BEST!"
"HOORAY FOR KARINA!"
"HELGA SHOULD WIN!"

"This is **fantastic** camouflage!" Trap said. "It will be tough to pick a winner."

Trap was right! All four contestants had done a **great job**. I wanted to vote for **Thora**, my crush, but how could I choose her when the others looked just as good?

Sven marched up to us. "**SO, WHO IS THE WINNER?**"

Trap and Ratilde shrugged. "We can't decide."

"Then it's up to **YOU**, Geronimo!" Sven shouted.

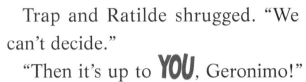

the crowd roared.

HIDING FROM THE DRAGONS

All the contestants **GLARED** at me, waiting for me to name the winner. Holey cheese, how could I choose?

So I just sat there, as quiet as a clam. The micekings quickly got annoyed.

"Well, smarty-mouse?"

"Who wins the Mega Challenge?"

"YEAH. WHICH SHIELD MOUSELET WINS?"

I began to stutter. "Well . . . I-I-I don't know . . . m-m-m-maybe . . ."

"Hurry up and decide, Geronimo!" Sven thundered, shaking his paw.

Just then the dragon alarm sounded.

TOO-TOOOT! TOO-TOOOOOOOOT!

A moment later, three dragons appeared in the sky, breathing fire. They swooped down over the village.

"Do you **sss**ee what I **sss**ee?" asked the first dragon.

"I **sss**ee a bunch of fresh meat, Red Fang," answered the second dragon. "How about you, **Sss**lither?"

"Me too, Broiler," said the third. "They **sss**eem juicy! Let's eat them up fa**sss**t!"

Red Fang, the RED dragon, landed right next to me and snapped at my tail. "What ta**sss**ty miceking flesh! It'**sss** mine! I **sss**aw it fir**sss**t!"

RED FANG

Red Fang is a dragon in the Devourer family. Devourers like to quickly barbecue micekings and eat them. For some reason, Red Fang seems to always be hungry for me!

I ran away and **ducked** behind the straw target.

"**Sss**o you want to play hide-and-**sss**eek, little mou**sss**eking?" Red Fang asked.

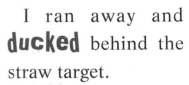 **1 WHOOSH!** He shot *FLAMES* at the target, reducing it to ashes and revealing my hiding place! So I **DASHED** under the cooking challenge table, taking refuge there.

2 WHOOSH! Red Fang unleashed his hot breath, and

MELTED CHEESE

flowed down on me like lava!

Finally, I crawled under the judges' table . . . but Red Fang found me there, too!

3 He **sniffed** the air, noticing the smell of the **Logi pepper** garland strung across the table. Then he smiled.

"What luck!" he cried. "With a **sss**ingle

I'm doomed!

flame, I'll have miceking meat with roa**SSS**ted **SSS**picy pepper**SSS**!"

He inhaled, getting ready to *BLAST* me with flames again.

This was it. I was going to be cooked, fried, Done!

"**HEEEELP!**" I screamed. "I don't want to become dinner for a dragon!"

We'll Be Back!

"Load the catapults! **RELEASE!**" Sven the Shouter commanded.

Just in time, something **slimy** hit Red Fang's head.

PLOP! PLOP! PLOP!

Bales of **MUD** mixed with hay rained down on the three dragons.

Slither swallowed one by mistake and spit

Yikes!

it out. "Let'**SSS** get out of
here!"

RED FANG grabbed the Logi
peppers. "For now, I'll take these!"
he growled.

Then he  off. "I
will be back with
King Gobbler
and his
army!" he
promised.

"Gather around, **MICEKINGS**!" Sven the Shouter yelled. "We must prepare for —" **BONK!** His wife, Mousehilde, **BOPPED** him on the head with her rolling pin.

"This is **YOUR FAULT**!" she said. "I told you to leave one mouseking **guarding** the catapults during the competition. That

is how the dragons were able to get so close to us!"

The villagers were scared.

"What do we do now, BRAVE Sven?" one rodent asked.

"Yes, courageous Sven, we don't have much time," said another.

Thora spoke up. "The **dragons** will be returning soon. We must **organize** our defense."

Sven nodded. "Well said, Thora. All the micekings must prepare for **BATTLE**! Copper, bring out the weapons."

Then Sven looked at me, and I tiptoed backward. I had a **bad feeling** all of a sudden.

Come with me!

"You come with me, **smarty-mouseking**," he said, grabbing me by the shoulders.

"Who? M-m-me?" I stuttered.

"Yes!" Sven replied. "We will go find **Loki Longsight**, the village soothsayer, and we'll ask

for advice. He can look in his book of **Dragon Lore and Legends** and tell us the best way to defeat them."

It wasn't a bad idea, actually. Sven and I headed to the soothsayer's **CAVE**, followed by all the micekings in the village.

THEY TOOK LOKI LONGSIGHT!

Sven stopped in front of the cave door. "**LOKI LONGSIGHT, OPEN UP!**" he shouted. "Sven the Shouter commands you!"

The micekings all cried out,

"SO SAYS SVEN THE SHOUTER!"

But Loki didn't answer.

Sven shouted even louder. "Hey, open up, **soothsayer**!"

I tugged on Sven's cloak. "Chief, the door to the cave is **half-open**," I told him.

"Why didn't you say that in the first place, **blubber brain**?" Sven asked. "Quick, get in there!"

I slowly pushed open the door. "L-Loki, are you there?" I asked.

Loki still didn't answer.

"Are you waiting for **groundhogs** to wake from their hibernation, smarty-mouseking? I said get in there!" Sven barked.

I stepped inside the cave, but I didn't see Loki. "He's not here!" I said.

1 I *RAN* back out and slipped on something **slimy**.

"Squeak!"

2 When I tried to get up, I **SLIPPED** a second time and fell right on my tail! *"OWWWW!"*

Oops!

SWIIIISHHHH

1

3 I **slid** right up to Sven's feet. He stared at me. "What do you mean he's **NOT HERE**? Where is he, then?"

I had no idea!

"I don't know!" I replied. "He didn't leave a **note**."

Thea, meanwhile, was examining the **STINKY SLIME** I had stepped on.

Help!

Well?

Yikes!

"Brave Sven, this is **DRAGON DROOL**!" she announced.

Sven sniffed it himself. "You're right! And I see some **RED SCALES** in there!"

"**Crusty codfish!**" I cried. "That scale belongs to **RED FANG**, the dragon who wants to roast and eat me! He must have taken Loki Longsight!"

"There's no time to waste!" Sven shouted, pumping his paw in the air. "We must **FIND HIM** quickly!"

All the micekings began to **volunteer** for the mission.

"CHOOSE ME, BRAVE LEADER!"

"I WILL GO! I'M THE STRONGEST!"

"PICK ME! I AM NOT AFRAID OF DRAGONS!"

Sven shook his head. "Since **GERONIMO** knows all about Red Fang, I will send him to find Loki Longsight."

"B-b-but . . ." I stammered.

Trap **BOLDLY** stepped forward. "I will go with Geronimo. Don't worry, Chief! We won't **disappoint** you!"

Sven nodded. "Well said, Trap! Bring the soothsayer back to Mouseborg and you will both receive **the greatest honor** in our village: a **MICEKING HELMET**!"

"That's nice, but I, er, have some very **urgent business** to attend to . . ." I said.

49

"No excuses, smarty-mouse!" Sven shouted. "You're leaving right now, and that's an order!"

"SO SAYS SVEN THE SHOUTER!"

everyone cried.

My paws began to tremble like jellyfish.

I was about to run away when . . .

"You can do it, Geronimo!"

It was Thora! She was cheering me on! Then my nephew Benjamin piped up.

"I **BELIEVE** in you, Uncle Ger!"

"GO GET 'EM, Geronimo!" Thea said.

Squeak! My friends and family gave me **courage**. I would find **Loki**. I would face the dragon. And I might even get my first miceking helmet!

THE HILLS OF WISE WORDS

Trap and I left Mouseborg.

"That dragon has left us a trail of STINKY drool, RED scales, and **roasted** trees," Trap remarked happily as we headed north. "This mission will be super easy!"

SUPER EASY?

We were on our way to face a FIERCE and terrible dragon with an appetite for micekings. What was *easy* about that?

But we had no choice. We had to SAVE Loki Longsight!

We followed the dragon's trail until we arrived at the very top of the TALLEST of the Hills of Wise Words. We could hear birds

twittering in the trees. Everything seemed peaceful until . . .

GUUUUUUUUUURGLE!

A deep sound echoed through the hills.

I jumped into Trap's arms.

"**IT'S THE DRAGONS!**" I squealed.

Trap chuckled. "Relax! That's just my stomach. I'm so hungry I could eat STALE CHEESE!"

We followed Red Fang's trail down a path. Then Trap stopped. "Look here, Geronimo!"

He pointed under a rock to a stash of **fjordberries** and truffles.

Trap started to *grab* them. "What a find! Want some, Cousin?"

"B-b-but they might belong to someone," I replied nervously. "**Leave them alone!**"

But Trap didn't listen.

Suddenly, I noticed some **strange tracks** in the dirt.

What strange tracks . . .

"Trap, these tracks look **suspicious**!" I said.

Trap **gobbled** down some berries and then walked over to me. He leaned over and looked at the tracks in the dirt.

"Hmm, you're right, Geronimo,"

Yummy!

he said. "These don't look like dragon tracks. They're too small."

"That's what worries me," I said. I glanced up at the rocks behind Trap, and my FUR stood on end.

"They look like the tracks of a **M-M-MEGA BOAR**!" I stammered.

MEGA BOAR

With its curved tusks and fierce hunger, the mega boar is a very, very aggressive wild boar! It digs in the dirt in search of roots and truffles, but when hungry, it will devour anything in its path. Caution: Never touch its food supply, or there will be trouble!

"How can you be so sure, smarty-mouseking?" Trap asked me.

"I-I'm sure," I stuttered, "because there is one **RIGHT BEHIND YOU**!"

Trap turned to see the HAIRY mega boar staring at us with FEROCIOUS eyes. We had stumbled upon its food supply!

GREAT SALTY SARDINES, we were in big trouble!

"What do we do?" I wailed.

Trap's **paws** were still full of fruit and truffles. "Let's scram, Geronimo! Hold on to your tail and

RUUUUUUN!"

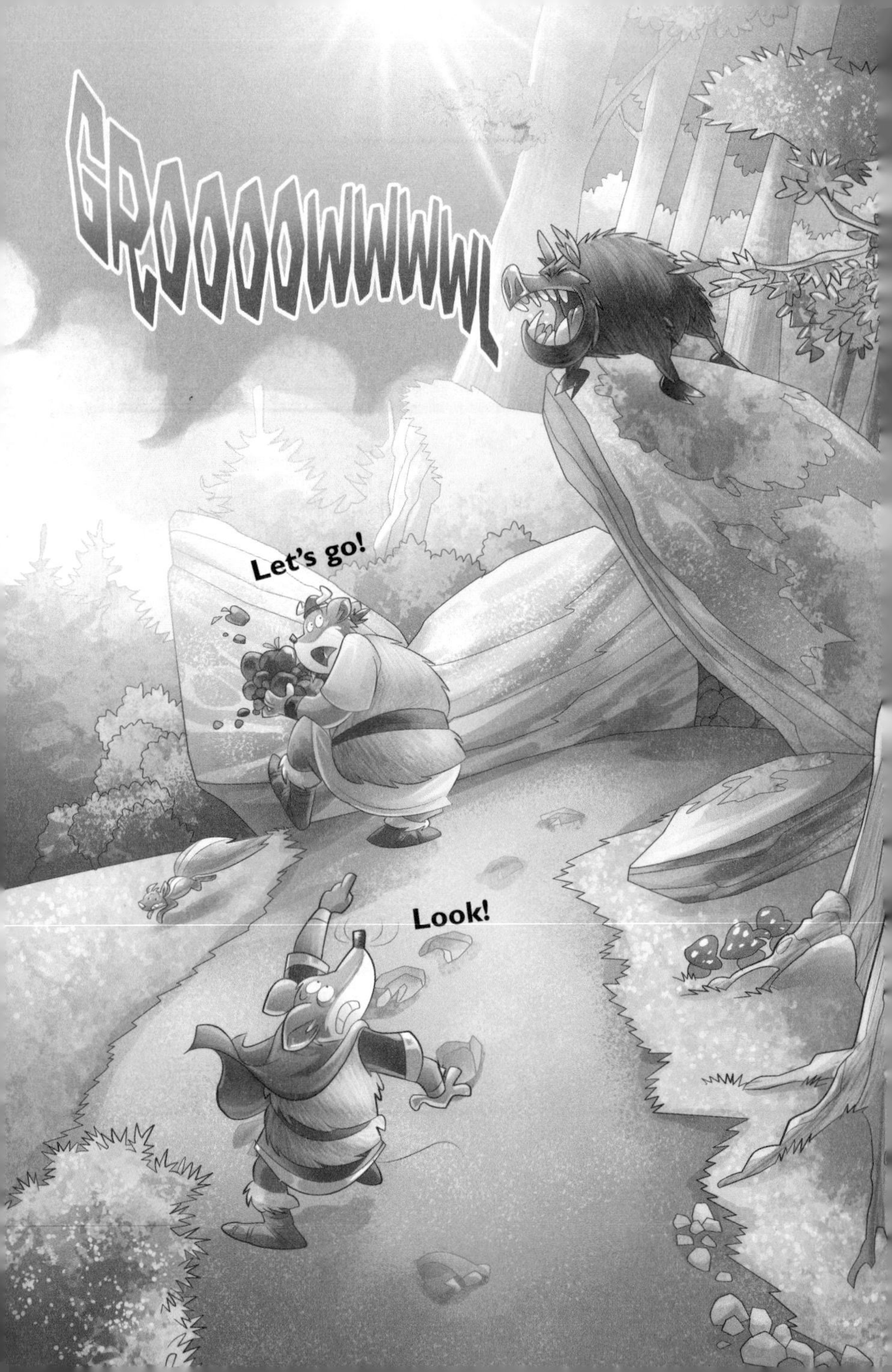
GROOOOWWWWL
Let's go!
Look!

WATCH YOUR FUR, GERONIMO!

Trap and I took off at *TOP SPEED* through the hills, followed by the mega boar.

We moved *FASTER* than a wheel of cheese rolling down a steep hill. We had to! The boar **GNASHED** its teeth as it ran, ready to **GOBBLE** us up! Everybody knows that you can't **MESS WITH** a mega boar's food supply — everybody but Trap, that is.

Then I realized something. "Are you still holding the boar's **FOOD**?" I asked Trap.

"Of course! It's **delicious**! Want some?" Trap asked.

"Why . . . *huff* . . . do you still have it . . . *puff*?" I asked, out of breath from running.

"Pant . . . give it back!"

Trap realized he had no choice. "Good-bye, sweet food!" he cried.

He tossed the food behind him — and it **HIT** the mega boar in the face! The beast was even **ANGRIER** now.

"*FASTER!*" I yelled.

We **ZIGZAGGED** between fallen tree branches and thorny bushes. Then a very **stinky** smell hit our snouts.

"That smell can only be **DRAGON DROOL**!" Trap cried.

We had a mega boar behind us, and we were heading right toward a terrible dragon!

WE WERE DOOMED!

The mega boar was on our tails. We kept running . . . and then we **slipped** in a puddle of dragon drool.

Now we were **EVEN MORE DOOMED**!

But just as the boar's tusks were about

to skewer us, a FLAME shot over our heads.

The mega boar yelped, turned around, and **RAN AWAY**.

One THREAT was gone . . . but another was in the bushes right in front of us.

SHOOOOSH

We're doomed!

Uh-oh!

RED FANG glared at us with his scary yellow eyes!

"Is it you again?" he asked. "Come clo**sss**er! That way I can eat you in a **sss**ingle bite!"

I began to shiver from the tip of my tail to the ends of my whiskers. Then I felt Trap pull me by the arm. He dragged me behind a large TREE TRUNK.

"Get over here, **SHRIMP**!" Red Fang roared, and he lunged toward us.

Then something unexpected happened.

Red Fang suddenly **RoaReD** in pain. Smoke puffed out of his nostrils, and he **TOPPLED OVER** with a boom.

I **PEEKED** out from my hiding place and saw the problem: One of his wings was caught in a thorny bush. He couldn't move or fly.

I took a deep breath. I might not be a **BRAVE** mouseking, but Trap and I had come to save **Loki Longsight**. I knew what I had to do. I stepped out from behind the tree branch and **slowly** walked toward the dragon.

"What happened?" I asked him.

"None of your bu**SSS**ine**SSS**, no**SSS**y mou**SSS**eking!" Red Fang roared. "I will roa**SSS**t you in a **SSS**plit **SSS**econd and crush you with my jaw**SSS**!"

He spat out a huge flame. I jumped back behind the tree branch to avoid it.

"That's it! I'm done!" I squealed.

Red Fang was **STUCK**. Trap and I could go back to the village without losing our fur.

But if we did that, we'd be leaving behind poor Loki. (Not to mention, I would NEVER get my miceking helmet!)

"You **FAILED** again, smarty-mouseking!" Sven the Shouter would say.

Then it hit me. I *was* a smarty-mouseking. I could think of a way to use Red Fang's predicament to our advantage.

I had an idea.

I walked right up to the dragon's face and began to squeak.

"L-L-LET'S MAKE A DEAL BETWEEN MOUSEKING AND DRAGON!"

THE SECRET DEAL
WITH RED FANG

Red Fang sniffed me. "Are you out of your furry head? I could eat you right now!"

Trap JUMPED out of our hiding place. "Geronimo, what are you thinking?" he asked.

"I mu**SSS**t admit, I am curiou**SSS**," Red Fang said. "No mou**SSS**eking has ever approached me like thi**SSS** before. What deal do you propo**SSS**e, shrimp?"

I took another deep breath.

"W-w-well, Trap and I could FREE you from the thorns," I began.

Red Fang looked interested. "Go on," he said.

70

"And then you could t-t-tell us where you've hidden our soothsayer, Loki Longsight," I continued.

"And promise not to gobble us up on the spot!" Trap added quickly.

Red Fang began to snicker. Then he snorted. Then he laughed so hard that the ground shook beneath our feet! My whiskers almost fell off in fright!

"Bad idea, Geronimo," Trap whispered. "We're about to become dinner for a dragon!"

Red Fang laughed so

hard that he became even more tangled in the thorny bush. He R©ARED out in pain.

"GRRRRRRRRRRRRRR!"

I knew Red Fang couldn't **REFUSE** our help now. "You can't fly, or even move," I said bravely. "Let us help you."

Red Fang scowled. "Very well!" he hissed. "We will make thi**sss** deal. But it mu**sss**t be kept a **sss**ecret!"

I quickly pulled out some parchment and my goose-feather pen (which I always carry with me, like a good scholar) and wrote out our deal.

I signed it, and then Red Fang grabbed the pen in his CLAW and signed, too.

After Red Fang signed, Trap and I carefully

removed the *thorny* branch from his wing.

SECRET DRAGON-MOUSEKING AGREEMENT*

I, Geronimo Stiltonord, will free Red Fang from the branch that hurt his wing.

In exchange, Red Fang of the Devourers of Beastgard will tell us everything he knows about Loki Longsight's whereabouts. And above all, he promises not to gobble up any micekings present.

GERONIMO

* The original was written in miceking runes, but it has been translated so you can read it!

Red Fang GRINNED and stretched out his wings. Then he eyed me **hungrily** as if I were a tasty treat.

HELMETS AND HERRING, I WAS ONE SCARED MOUSEKING!

But I held the parchment agreement in front of me like a SHIELD. "You p-p-promised not to **hurt** us!" I reminded him. "And you must RETURN Loki Longsight to us!"

"I don't know any Loki Long**sss**ight," Red Fang replied. "The only fresh mou**sss**emeat here is you two!"

"We found your DROOL and one of your RED SCALES outside his cave!" I protested. "What did you do with him?"

"That wa**sss**n't me!" Red Fang repeated.

"What do you mean?" I asked.

"After you mice attacked u**sss**, I wa**sss**

74

SSSo hungry that I **gobbled** up the Logi pepper**SSS**," Red Fang explained. "We dragon**SSS** need them to help create our **FIERY** breath."

I shuddered, thinking about how Red Fang's flames had almost roasted me before.

"But they were **TOO HOT**, even for me!" the dragon continued. "I **SSS**tarted to **cough** and drool!"

"Then what happened?" Trap asked.

"My eye**SSS** were **WATERING** badly," Red Fang replied. "I couldn't **SSS**ee where I wa**SSS** going, and I flew into a cave."

Trap and I looked at each other. "Loki Longsight's cave!" we both guessed.

"I didn't **SSS**ee a mou**SSS**eking in there," Red Fang said. "I waited until my eye**SSS** **SSS**topped watering, and then I *FLEW* away."

Trap's eyes narrowed. "You mean you didn't take our soothsayer? Or **gobble** him up?"

Red Fang shook his head. "If I had eaten him, would my empty belly be GROWLING like thi**sss**?"

He patted his big **red** belly, and it made a noise:

GUUUUURGLE!

I couldn't believe it. We had been CHASED by a mega boar and FACED a deadly dragon to find Loki Longsight — all for nothing!

"Becau**SSS**e of our deal, I will let you e**SSS**cape," Red Fang continued. "But I will return to your village with an army of dragon**SSS**. And then I will eat you raw, ju**SSS**t as you are!"

Then he flapped his wings and **FLEW OFF**.

Trap slapped me on the back. "Good work, Cousin! You saved us from being **toasted** like a cheese sandwich!"

"But we still haven't found Loki Longsight," I said. "We should keep

LOOKING for him."

"No way!" Trap said. "We have to go back to Mouseborg and **WARN** the village about the dragon attack."

Let's find Loki!

We have to warn the village!

DRAGON ATTACK!

I knew Trap was right. We raced toward Mouseborg like LIGHTNING.

Sven the Shouter started SHOUTING as soon as he saw us. "Are you CHEESEHEADS back already? Where is Loki Longsight?"

"W-w-we . . . um . . . d-didn't find him, Chief," I stuttered.

"How dare you return with EMPTY PAWS!" Sven shouted so loudly that it ruffled my fur.

Suddenly, the dragon alarm rang throughout the village.

Before you could say **cheese**, the sky became filled with dragons. Their leader, **Gobbler the Putrid**, flew at the front of the pack.

Gobbler wore the Crown of the Seven Rubies, forged in volcanic lava.

"Look at the**sss**e ta**sss**ty miceking

GOBBLER
the Putrid

Gobbler the Putrid is the unchallenged leader of the dragons. He smells so bad even flies stay away from him! He's always in a bad mood and always very hungry. His favorite food is fresh miceking stew.

morsel**SSS**!" he called out to his followers.

Sven turned to the micekings. "Load the catapults!

AIM!
ATTAAAAACK!"

Gobbler called his dragons to action. "Follow me, my winged **SSS**ubject**SSS**!

DIVE,
DIVE, DIVE!"

This time, the dragons were **ready** for our miceking defenses. They batted away the **STICKY** mud balls with their tails.

They blew **FLAMES** onto the straw roofs of our houses, setting them on fire!

Some micekings **RAN** for their weapons.

Others ran away from the flames. I was headed for the catapults when I heard something **thundering** behind me that made my whiskers curl with fear.

GRRRRRROWWWWWL!

Shivering squids, that roar was close — TOO CLOSE!

I turned and came face-to-face with a dragon with R∈D scales, pointy fangs, SHARP claws, and one injured wing . . . **RED FANG**! He and I had made a deal — but now the deal was off!

Red Fang looked like he was going to keep his promise to *eat me raw*!

SQUEAK!

He landed right in front of me.

"**Sss**tay away!" he called to the other

dragons. "Thi**sss** shrimpy mou**sss**eking is all mine!"

HORNS AND THORNS!

My whiskers trembled with fright. The end was near! Red Fang was going to devour me, and there was nothing I could do about it. I was doomed!

You Can't Hide from Me, Mouseking!

Red Fang *LUNGED* at me. I was so afraid that I couldn't move a muscle!

Then Trap took me by the **paw**.

"Get out of there, Geronimo!" he yelled, *DRAGGING* me under the stage.

Let's scram!

Okay!

Red Fang followed us. "You can't hide! I will **SSS**till **SSS**natch you!"

We <u>flattened</u> ourselves against the ground. The dragon plunged his claws into the wooden boards above us. Then he smacked the stage with his heavy, **SPIKED** tail.

Squeak!

Found you!

The stage was now full of more **holes** than a slice of Swiss!

We were about to be **fried**, roasted, and **TOASTED**!

Trap held me tightly. "I've always loved you, Cousin!" He sobbed. "You're the **BRAVEST** smarty-mouseking I know!"

This is it, I thought. *Good-bye, Mouseborg, my hometown! Good-bye, lovely Thora! Good-bye, miceking world!*

A **FIREBALL** formed in Red Fang's throat, but before he could release it . . .

It's over!

We're cooked!

"Get out of here, you ugly lizard face!"

Fjords and fishbones, it was Thora! As she bravely ran toward the stage, she took a SHARP shell comb out of her hair and flung it toward the dragon's face. The blow stunned Red Fang.

"GREAT SHOT, you amazing Shield Mouselet!" Trap cheered.

Take that!

Red Fang flew off, and Trap shivered.

"That was c-c-close," he said.

I stared at Thora with admiration. "Brave Thora, you've SAVED our fur!" I squeaked.

Then I saw that she wasn't alone. **THEA**, **HELGA**, and **Karina** all stood behind her.

And behind them stood all the other Shield Mouselets in the village! They had joined forces to organize an **anti-dragon** defense.

OH, WHAT FABUMOUSE MICEKINGS!

THE CHARGE OF THE SHIELD MOUSELETS

The Shield Mouselets' defense took the **dragons** by surprise with a charge of unexpected weapons:

1. Heavy cauldrons filled with **stinky food** from the cooking challenge.
2. Catapults loaded with **sharp shells** from the shell challenge.
3. Buckets of **CLEAN WATER** because dragons can't stand it — water washes away their stench!
4. Fishing nets that doubled as **dragon-catching nets!**

SWEET SARDINES!

SHIELD MOUSELETS TO THE RESCUE!

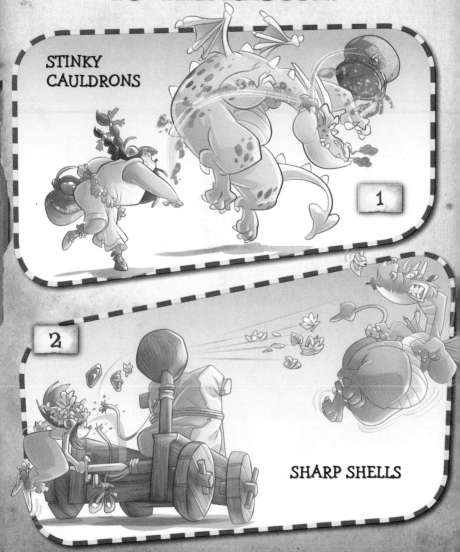

STINKY CAULDRONS

1

2

SHARP SHELLS

These Shield Mouselets were a **FORCE** to be reckoned with!

They **flung** the cauldrons with amazing force. They **hurled** the sharp shells with precise aim. They worked together to **stun** the dragons and then **CAPTURE** them in nets. It was miceking poetry in action!

Gobbler the Putrid tried to get his dragons in order.

"Dragon**SSS**, get in formation! Claw**SSS** out!" he yelled.

But they could not stop the Shield Mouselets.

"Get out of here, you scaly scoundrels!" Thea yelled.

"Beat it, you lousy beasts!" the others joined in.

Gobbler continued to call out orders. But his **DRENCHED** and battered dragons did

not want to fight anymore. The Shield Mouselets were too much for them!

Finally, Gobbler gave in. "**RETREAT!**" he yelled.

Ow! Ow!

Yuck! Clean water!

Retreat!

Before flying off, Red Fang fixed his **FIERY** eyes on me. "You managed to e**SSS**cape thi**SSS** time, mou**SSS**eking! But next time, I will roa**SSS**t you for dinner!"

A wave of **relief** washed over me as I watched him and the other dragons **disappear** over the horizon.

FOR NOW, WE WERE ALL SAFE!

KNOCK! KNOCK! ANYONE THERE?

The dragon attack was over — and it was all thanks to the village's **SHIELD MOUSELETS**!

"Rodents of **Mouseborg**, rejoice!" Sven shouted. "The dragons have fled!"

"**WE WON!**" squealed the micekings.

"Hooray for the Shield mouselets!"

"**DOWN WITH THE DRAGONS!**"

"Hip, hip, hooray for the Shield Mouselets!"

"We will celebrate!" Sven announced. "My wife, Mousehilde, will prepare a fabumouse **banquet** and —"

Mousehilde interrupted her husband's speech by **BOPPING** him on the head. "Aren't you **forgetting** something? We can't celebrate until we find **Loki Longsight**! He's still missing!"

100

Sven pointed at me. "Geronimo, finding him was YOUR JOB! Tell us what happened!"

"SO SAYS SVEN THE SHOUTER!"

the micekings cried.

"Well," I began. "First, Trap and I tracked RED FANG . . ."

"OOOOOOOOOOOOOH!" the micekings exclaimed.

"But we didn't find Loki Longsight or any sign of him," I finished.

"NOOOOOOOOOOOO!" the micekings squeaked.

I couldn't tell them about my deal with the dragon. It was a SECRET! All the micekings knew was that I had failed.

Thea came to my rescue. "Let's go back to Loki's CAVE and search for more clues," she suggested.

"Thea is right!" Trap said loudly. "Let's go!"

I truly have a **fabumouse** family. They always stand up for me!

So we all returned to the cave. We **SEARCHED** everywhere around it. We climbed trees. We LOOKED under bushes.

Where is he?

Look everywhere!

Hmm . . .

I'll find him . . .

We even lifted up boulders! (Well, I didn't, but micekings with **big muscles** did.) But there was **no trace** of Loki Longsight!

I put my snout to the ground to look for tracks — and **bumped** right into the cave's front door. "**OW!**" I cried.

Then I realized something. I had just bumped into a **CLUE**! "**HELMETS AND HERRING**, the cave door is closed!" I cried.

"Are you **SURE** you didn't close it with your snout, smarty-mouseking?" Sven asked me.

"I'm sure," I replied.

"Then who **CLOSED** it?" Sven asked.

Then it hit me. "Maybe Loki returned to his **CAVE** while we were **fighting** the dragons! He could be in there right now," I said.

There was only **ONE WAY** to find out.

"Loki Longsight!" Sven shouted at the top of his lungs. "ARE YOU IN THERE, soothsayer?"

There was no reply — but then a stone fell out of the window above the door. A piece of parchment was tied to the stone.

"It must be from Loki!" I realized.

"Then read it, smarty-mouseking!" Sven bellowed.

I unrolled the parchment and read the words aloud: *The soothsayer is only in on days when the moon is full . . . in months beginning with the letter J . . . and not during mealtimes! Please come back another time.*

Have I already told you that Sven is called "the Shouter" because he shouts **VERY, VERY, VERY LOUDLY**? Well, when he gets **angry**, he shouts even louder! And this time he was **angrier** than I had ever seen him.

"Where did you disappear to?" Sven bellowed. "Answer me!"

"SO SAYS SVEN THE SHOUTER!"

Answer me!

the micekings sang out.

The soothsayer tossed another **STONE** out the window, with a new message attached.

I read it out loud: *"I went out to search for honey, mouse grass, and fjordberries. What do you want?"*

Angry, the other micekings started shouting at Loki.

What are you talking about?

"Didn't you hear the **dragon alarm**?"

"Didn't you smell their **TERRIBLE STENCH**?"

"Didn't you see the *FIERY FLAMES*?"

Another note *FLEW* out the window:

"What dragons? I didn't see a single scale. Not a single fang."

It was no use arguing. Our soothsayer was supposed to be good at **SEEING** the future. But this time, he hadn't even seen what was **RIGHT OUTSIDE** his cave!

AND THE WINNER IS . . .

We returned to the village.

"Loki is found! Let the **banquet** begin!" Sven shouted. "Mousehilde will make delicious **gloog** for all!"

"HOORAY FOR MOUSEHILDE! HOORAY FOR GLOOG!"

the micekings cheered.

Gloog is traditional **miceking stew**, and Mousehilde's is the best!

That night, the village **celebrated** with a great feast of gloog, Stenchberg **CHEESE**, finnbrew (the official drink of micekings), and other miceking specialties.

108

Just as I was about to take my first **bite**, Sven interrupted me.

"What are you doing, smarty-mouseking?" he asked.

"I-I-I'm **eating**," I sputtered.

Sven held up a paw. "**S+⊚P** right there! First you must announce the winner of the **Shield Mouselet Mega Challenge**!"

The micekings began to chant.

"**CHOOSE A WINNER!
CHOOSE A WINNER!
CHOOSE A WINNER!**"

Crusty codfish, what was I supposed to do? I tried to think of a way out. "L-l-let's **THINK** about this, Sven," I stuttered. "Red Fang ate the **hot pepper** sash that gets awarded to the winner, so there is no way to . . ."

"I've got an **extra**, Smarty-mouse!" Sven cried, **TOSSING** another sash made of Logi peppers at me.

I turned paler than **MOZZARELLA**. I had no more excuses!

Shivering squids, I didn't know who to choose!

I wanted to choose **Thora**, who had saved me from **RED FANG** . . .

But there was also my sister, **THEA** . . .

And **HELGA** . . .

And Karina . . .

They all deserved to win. Squeak!

Then Mousehilde walked up and took the sash from me. "Forget it, Geronimo! All the **SHIELD MOUSELETS** in the village have made a decision. For fighting with GREAT SKILL and saving the village . . . all four are winners!"

"WE'RE ALL WINNERS!" the contestants cheered.

When the Shield Mouselets make a decision, no rodent **argues** with them! The other micekings began to clap and cheer.

"HIP, HIP, HOORAY FOR THE WINNERS!"

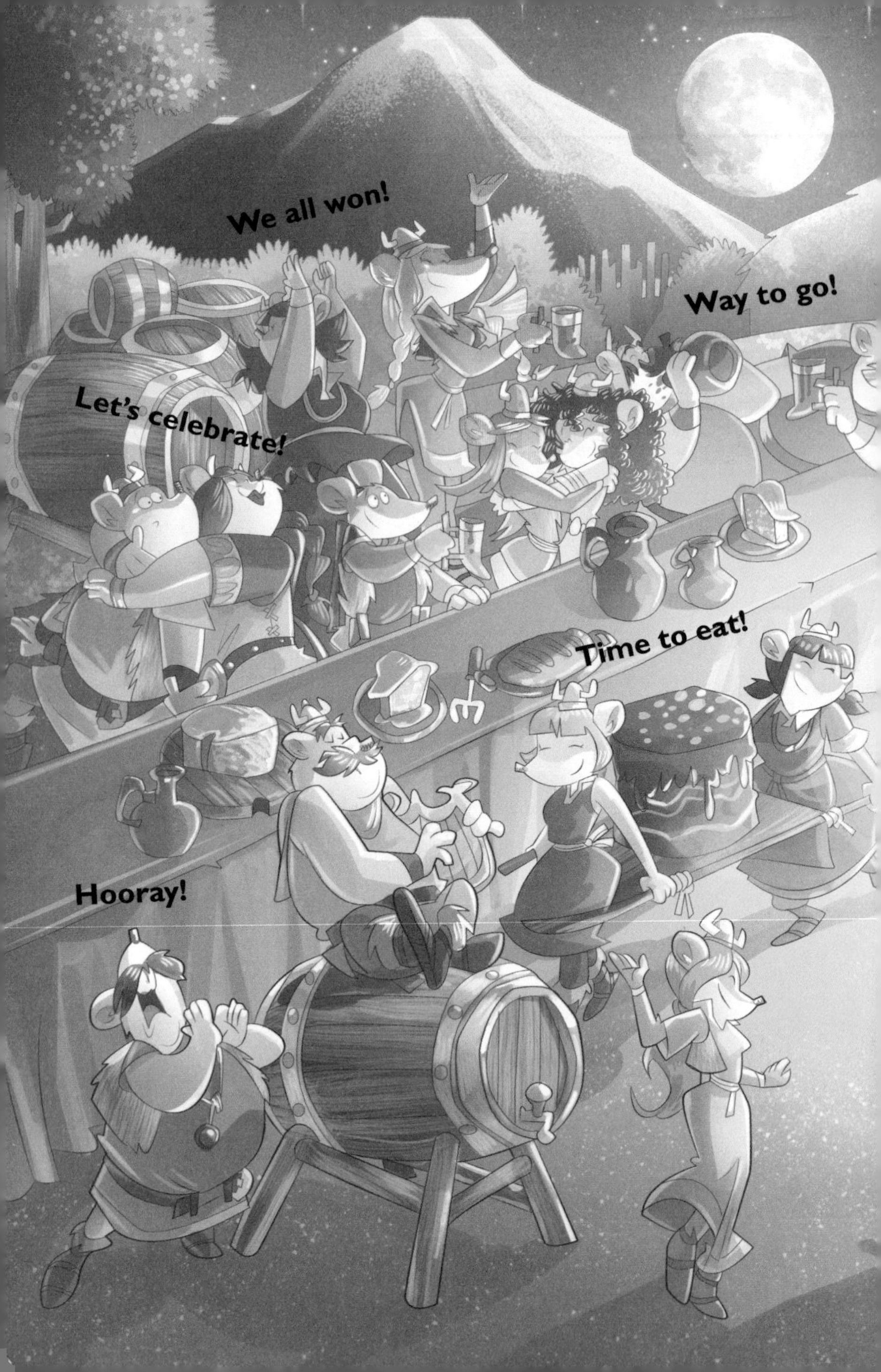
We all won!
Way to go!
Let's celebrate!
Time to eat!
Hooray!

Hooray for the micekings!
Yay!
We're all winners!
Three cheers!
Hooray!

Then Sven gave each of the four Shield Mouselets a special **MICEKING HELMET** for driving off the dragons.

"SO SAYS SVEN THE SHOUTER!"

the villagers cried.

And then (at last), we were able to eat!

It really was a **fabumouse** feast, and when every crumb was eaten, the micekings broke out into *festive dancing* around the banquet table. By the time I went home and slipped under the covers, I was as happy as a CLAM in its shell.

I was so **proud** of the Shield Mouselets for working together. And even though I hadn't earned a **MICEKING HELMET** yet, I was still happy. I had made a secret pact with a dragon — and lived to **NOT** tell a soul about it (because it's a **SECRET**!). So I was content. Plus, I knew that I would earn a **MICEKING HELMET** sooner or later!

But that's another miceking story for another day!

Good night!

MICEKING ISLAND

Beastgard

Gullet Valley

Feargard

Forest of a
Thousand
Scales

Oofadale

Yawning
Cove

Helpful Hills

Mouseborg

Don't miss any adventures of the Micekings!

#1 Attack of the Dragons

#2 The Famouse Fjord Race

#3 Pull the Dragon's Tooth!

#4 Stay Strong, Geronimo!

Up Next:

#5 The Mysterious Message

Be sure to read all my fabumouse adventures!

#1 Lost Treasure of the Emerald Eye

#2 The Curse of the Cheese Pyramid

#3 Cat and Mouse in a Haunted House

#4 I'm Too Fond of My Fur!

#5 Four Mice Deep in the Jungle

#6 Paws Off, Cheddarface!

#7 Red Pizzas for a Blue Count

#8 Attack of the Bandit Cats

#9 A Fabumouse Vacation for Geronimo

#10 All Because of a Cup of Coffee

#11 It's Halloween, You 'Fraidy Mouse!

#12 Merry Christmas, Geronimo!

#13 The Phantom of the Subway

#14 The Temple of the Ruby of Fire

#15 The Mona Mousa Code

#16 A Cheese-Colored Camper

#17 Watch Your Whiskers, Stilton!

#18 Shipwreck on the Pirate Islands

#19 My Name Is Stilton, Geronimo Stilton

#20 Surf's Up, Geronimo!

#21 The Wild, Wild West

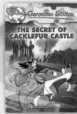

#22 The Secret of Cacklefur Castle

A Christmas Tale

#23 Valentine's Day
Disaster

#24 Field Trip to
Niagara Falls

#25 The Search for
Sunken Treasure

#26 The Mummy
with No Name

#27 The Christmas
Toy Factory

#28 Wedding
Crasher

#29 Down and Out
Down Under

#30 The Mouse Island
Marathon

#31 The Mysterious
Cheese Thief

Christmas Catastrophe

#32 Valley of the
Giant Skeletons

#33 Geronimo and the
Gold Medal Mystery

#34 Geronimo Stilton,
Secret Agent

#35 A Very Merry
Christmas

#36 Geronimo's
Valentine

#37 The Race Across
America

#38 A Fabumouse
School Adventure

#39 Singing Sensation

#40 The Karate Mouse

#41 Mighty Mount
Kilimanjaro

#42 The Peculiar
Pumpkin Thief

#43 I'm Not a
Supermouse!

#44 The Giant
Diamond Robbery

#45 Save the White
Whale!

#46 The Haunted
Castle

#47 Run for the Hills, Geronimo!

#48 The Mystery in Venice

#49 The Way of the Samurai

#50 This Hotel Is Haunted!

#51 The Enormouse Pearl Heist

#52 Mouse in Space!

#53 Rumble in the Jungle

#54 Get into Gear, Stilton!

#55 The Golden Statue Plot

#56 Flight of the Red Bandit

Special Edition!

The Hunt for the Golden Book

#57 The Stinky Cheese Vacation

#58 The Super Chef Contest

#59 Welcome to Moldy Manor

Special Edition!

The Hunt for the Curious Cheese

#60 The Treasure of Easter Island

#61 Mouse House Hunter

#62 Mouse Overboard!

Special Edition!

The Hunt for the Secret Papyrus

#63 The Cheese Experiment

#64 Magical Mission

#65 Bollywood Burglary

Special Edition!

The Hunt for the Hundredth Key

#66 Operation: Secret Recipe

Don't miss any of my special edition adventures!

THE KINGDOM OF FANTASY

THE QUEST FOR PARADISE:
THE RETURN TO THE KINGDOM OF FANTASY

THE AMAZING VOYAGE:
THE THIRD ADVENTURE IN THE KINGDOM OF FANTASY

THE DRAGON PROPHECY:
THE FOURTH ADVENTURE IN THE KINGDOM OF FANTASY

THE VOLCANO OF FIRE:
THE FIFTH ADVENTURE IN THE KINGDOM OF FANTASY

THE SEARCH FOR TREASURE:
THE SIXTH ADVENTURE IN THE KINGDOM OF FANTASY

THE ENCHANTED CHARMS:
THE SEVENTH ADVENTURE IN THE KINGDOM OF FANTASY

THE PHOENIX OF DESTINY:
AN EPIC KINGDOM OF FANTASY ADVENTURE

THE HOUR OF MAGIC:
THE EIGHTH ADVENTURE IN THE KINGDOM OF FANTASY

THE WIZARD'S WAND:
THE NINTH ADVENTURE IN THE KINGDOM OF FANTASY

THE SHIP OF SECRETS:
THE TENTH ADVENTURE IN THE KINGDOM OF FANTASY

THE JOURNEY THROUGH TIME

BACK IN TIME:
THE SECOND JOURNEY THROUGH TIME

THE RACE AGAINST TIME:
THE THIRD JOURNEY THROUGH TIME

LOST IN TIME:
THE FOURTH JOURNEY THROUGH TIME

Dear mouse friends,
thanks for reading,

and good-bye until
the next book!